A Little Book of
Etiquette

Vijaya Kumar

NEW DAWN PRESS, INC.
Chicago • Slough • New Delhi

NEW DAWN PRESS GROUP

Published by New Dawn Press Group
New Dawn Press, Inc., 244 South Randall Rd # 90, Elgin, IL 60123

New Dawn Press, 2 Tintern Close, Slough, Berkshire, SL1-2TB, UK

New Dawn Press (An Imprint of Sterling Publishers (P) Ltd.)
A-59, Okhla Industrial Area, Phase-II, New Delhi-110020

A Little Book of Etiquette
Copyright © 2004, New Dawn Press
ISBN 1 932705 18 X
Reprint 2010

All rights are reserved. No part of this publication may be reproduced, stored in a retrieval system or transmitted, in any form or by any means, mechanical, photocopying, recording or otherwise, without prior written permission of the original publisher.

NOTE FROM THE PUBLISHER

The author specifically disclaims any liability, loss or risk whatsoever, which is incurred or likely to be incurred, as a consequence of any direct or indirect use of information given in this book. The contents of this work are a personal interpretation of the subject by the author.

PRINTED IN INDIA

Contents

Preface 4

Introduction 5

Home Etiquette 6

Dining Etiquette 12

Business Etiquette 30

Etiquette for Occasions 44

Saying the Right Thing 49

Demeanour and Poise 66

Correspondence 72

Games and Travel 81

Tidbits 91

Faux Pas 95

Preface

This book is by no means an extensive study by any professional. The data provided in this book are my own interpretations of the subject, gleaned from various books, and presented from a layperson's viewpoint.

The book deals with each aspect of the study, point by point, in a simple language, and serves as a ready reckoner for those who have no time to go through heavy, indepth studies.

The publishers and I hold no responsibility for any discrepancy in the script. We would welcome suggestions or intimation of errors that come to anybody's notice.

Vijaya Kumar

Introduction

Social traditions, based on courtesy, kindness and graciousness have been bequeathed to us in the form of etiquette. We desperately need to hold on to these valuable norms, and appreciate the changing times and styles of our dynamic society.

Even successful and experienced people are aware that they need information and counsel on social and business etiquette. This book presents tips on etiquette at home, business, special occasions, dining etiquette, responding to invitations and correspondence, games and travel, and demeanour and poise. Some facts and titbits, and also social blunders find expression here.

Home Etiquette

1. Children need to know all about etiquette at a young age to get them ready for the world.
2. What may sound cute at home may be received with considerably less tolerance elsewhere.
3. Rules are different for dealing with adults and dealing with peers or children.

The Basics

1. Be kind and civil.
2. Treat everybody with respect and politeness. If you treat someone with respect, that person too will do likewise.
3. Whenever possible try to share your joys and triumphs, losses and securities with your children who possess a basic, uncluttered wisdom.

Relations with Adults

1. Convince your children, who are afflicted with shyness to some degree, that everybody, regardless of age, is shy, to a certain extent, around new people or unfamiliar surroundings.
2. Children should be persuaded to stop worrying about themselves and focus on other people.
3. When children meet someone new, they should stand up.

4. They can either shake hands with the person or join both hands together and wish him 'namaste', they can even say 'hello' and smile.
5. Young people should be made aware of the fact that people like to talk about themselves, and so, during conversations, they should listen patiently.
6. People do not mind being asked questions, as long as they are not too personal or downright rude.
7. Teach your children to be observant, so that they become aware of the other person's interest like noticing a guitar, a tennis racquet, crayons, etc., and ask relevant questions to set the conversation going.
8. They should try not to interrupt, but rather listen carefully, unless something urgent turns up, in which case, they should say, "Excuse me."
9. When a child is offered a gift which is not to his liking, instead of grimacing or showing his displeasure, he should accept it graciously and thank the person warmly.
10. Teach your child to ask for assistance in a shop, rather than trying to attract the shopkeeper's attention by coughing, or clapping his hands, or drumming on the table, etc.
11. Your child should greet elders with deference, and address them properly with respect, like Uncle, Aunty, Mr, Mrs, Dr, Captain, Grandma or Grandpa, etc.
12. When the child introduces his teacher to his parents, the teacher's name is mentioned first.
13. While introducing someone to your parents, it helps to provide a little information about that person,

"This is my friend Ram. We are in the same class, but different sections."

14. When introducing dignitaries, they are mentioned first, as a respect for the offices they hold.

Table Manners

1. Parents should set a good example in table manners for their children.
2. Children should be taught the correct usage of cutlery – how to hold the fork, knife or spoon; in which hand to hold each, etc.
3. Once a piece of cutlery is lifted, it does not go back to the table, but is placed on the plate.
4. Do not ever wave cutlery around to make a point.
5. When a napkin is removed for use from the table, it should be placed on the lap, and not tucked under the chin.
6. Sit straight instead of slumping and keep the elbows off the table.
7. While chewing food, keep your mouth closed. Do not talk with food in your mouth.
8. Remember, it is bad manners to eat too fast in the company of others.
9. Never place any of your personal belongings like keys, purse, etc., on the table while eating.
10. While buttering a piece of toast, break it into bite-sized bits before buttering each piece.
11. If you happen to belch, say "excuse me" to no one in particular, and go on eating.

12. When you have guests for dinner, you have to be on your best behaviour, and see that your guests are served well.
13. If you are eating in someone else's house, or have guests in your house, do not reject food outright, but have a little to taste.
14. Always take only the right quantity of food that you know you can finish off, and avoid leaving any food on your plate.

Treatment of Guests

1. It is always a welcome sight for the visitors or guests to see their host/hostess at the door.
2. It would be courteous to help the guests with their luggage and show them to their room.
3. After indicating the location of the bathroom and toilet, you must immediately offer them refreshments.
4. Try to make your guests feel at home.
5. In case you do not have a spare bedroom to accommodate them, you can give them the children's room, or else place them in your own room (if they are there to stay for a while) instead of in the drawing-room.
6. These matters should be settled before the guests arrival.
7. Fresh flowers add to the character of the rooms.
8. Several refreshments during the day for the guests must be offered.

9. Before they retire for the night, you can ask them if they would like an early cup of morning tea.
10. In the process of preparing special dishes for them, do not spend all your time in the kitchen. It is bad manners to leave your guests on their own all day long.
11. When you take your guests sightseeing or shopping, courtesy demands that you pay for everything, except the shopping.
12. It would be courteous to give your guests some gifts, which can be simple, like some homemade pickles or jams, or else some utility item.

Visiting Others

1. When you go as a guest to someone else's house, always carry something for your host and hostess, or even their children, like fruits, toys, mementoes, etc.
2. If you have to share the room with your host's children, so be it. Do not make a fuss.
3. If you have reservations about certain types of food that you take, let you host know in advance.
4. Never invite your relatives or friends to meet you at your host's house; it would be better for you to visit them instead.
5. Avoid taking your pets with you.
6. You should be careful in handling your host's children. Avoid criticising or disciplining them.
7. Ensure that your own children behave well. Avoid unpleasantness.

8. Always keep the room you occupy neat and clean, with your bed made up, before you leave the room.
9. Offer your services to your host/hostess while they are engaged in cooking, washing dishes, laying the table, dusting, etc.
10. You can also offer to shop for groceries, fruit and vegetables, etc.
11. If you have to share the bathroom with your hosts family, wait till the school-going children and office-going people, who are rushed for time, have finished using it.
12. Avoid using the telephone, unless absolutely necessary, and then make it short, and offer to pay for it.
13. You may tip the servants at the end of your stay.
14. When you return home, etiquette demands that you send your host a simple thank-you card or note.

Dining Etiquette

Table Manners

1. Always sit straight, and keep your elbows off the table, preferable keeping your hands on your lap while not eating.
2. Never chew your food with your mouth open.
3. It is always good manners to swallow the food before speaking.
4. Do not gulp down your food. Not only is it unattractive, but also unhealthy.
5. Ensure that your keep pace with others, and not linger over your first course while the others are already waiting for their dessert.
6. When you find something stuck between your teeth, do not pick at it while at the table. You can excuse yourself for a while, and dislodge it in the bathroom.
7. Between courses, do not light up your cigarette, as it affects the others' taste buds, or it may be an irritant to them, especially if they are allergic to smoke.
8. Do not use a plate as an ash-tray.
9. See that your personal belongings like a wallet or purse, keys, spectacles, etc., are off the table.
10. Do not use the salt and pepper before tasting your food. This can be very offensive to the person who has cooked the meal and is seated amongst you.

11. Never blow on any hot liquid, but wait till it is cool enough for you to drink it.
12. Cut food that is just enough for the next mouthful, instead of stuffing your mouth with huge chunkfuls.
13. Always pass the food to the right, unless someone on your left specifically asks for a particular dish near you.
14. When you have finished eating, do not push your plate away.
15. Also make sure that you do not push your chair back.
16. If a person has some medicine after food, etiquette requires that you do not enquire about the reasons.
17. If inadvertently you belch, cover your mouth with a napkin and say "Excuse me" to no one in particular.
18. Avoid asking people where they are going once they leave the table.
19. When you want to butter your toast, take some of it on to your plate, and then spread it on the toast.
20. If you spill something, do not agitate or panic, but quietly blot up what you can.

Eating Gracefully

1. You can eat cake with the fingers if it is bite-sized, otherwise use the fork and spoon, with the spoon in your right hand for scooping it up.
2. When you squeeze a lime between the fingers, use the other hand to shield the lime squirt so that the diner beside you is not subjected to an eyeful of lemon juice.

3. Oranges and sweet limes can be peeled with a knife, and each segment of the fruit eaten with fingers.
4. When pineapple is cut into tiny pieces, use a spoon, else, use a fork.
5. While eating a watermelon, use a spoon. Put the seeds into the palm of your hand, and transfer them to the side of your plate.
6. Pasta, spaghetti or noodles should be eaten with a fork, twirling or coiling a few strands around the fork before eating them.
7. Food served on plantain leaves in South India requires eating with fingers.
8. Use a fork and knife for a *dosa* or an *uthappam*, with the knife in the right hand.
9. When *idli* or *vada* is served, use a spoon. First eat a small piece of *idli*, followed by a spoonful of chutney or *sambhar*.
10. Rice is generally eaten, using a fork and spoon.
11. Use your fingers to break *papads* into tiny bits as you eat.
12. Use your fingers while eating any kind of leavened bread, like roti, chapatti, *nan, puri*, etc.
13. Dry vegetables can be eaten, using a fork, while the gravied ones require a spoon.
14. *Kababs* and *cutlets* are eaten using a fork and knife.
15. Small pieces of boneless chicken can be eaten, using a fork. You can also use a knife.
16. Chicken with bones, or *tandoori* chicken are best eaten, using a fork and knife. Be careful while handling the greasy pieces.

17. Fish is generally eaten, using a fork and knife.
18. Cut the spring rolls into bite-sizes and use a fork to put them into your mouth.
19. Burgers, hotdogs and patties can be eaten, using your fingers.
20. Pizzas can be eaten, either using the fingers, or a fork.
21. For *pav bhaji*, use a knife and fork for the bread and a spoon for the vegetables.
22. Salads can be eaten, using a knife or fork.
23. Pastry can be eaten with fingers, or a fork and spoon.
24. When an omelette is served with toast, use a knife and fork, else use only a fork.
25. Sandwiches are easily handled by fingers.
26. Do not slurp while having soup.
27. Dessert can be eaten, using a dessertspoon or a small spoon, or even a fork, depending on the sweet served.
28. If you are resting between meals, cross your cutlery, the fork on top with prongs facing down.

The Use of Cutlery

1. When you use a fork and spoon, the former is held in the left hand while the latter is held in the right hand.
2. While using a knife and fork also, the fork is in the left hand, while the right hand is used for the knife for cutting.
3. At a sit-down meal, generally two pieces of cutlery are used at a time, though the other pieces are also laid out on the table.

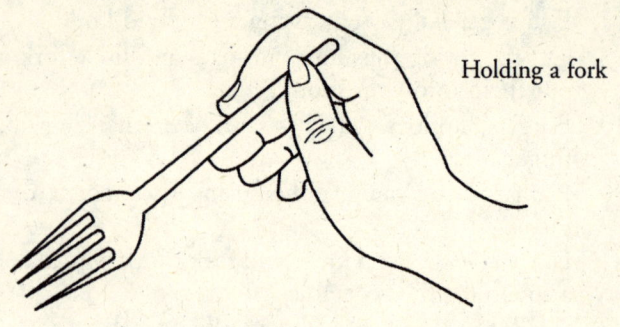

Holding a fork

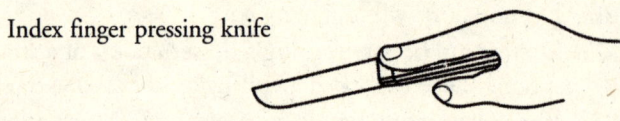

Index finger pressing knife

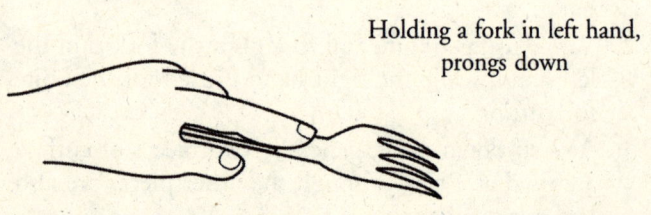

Holding a fork in left hand, prongs down

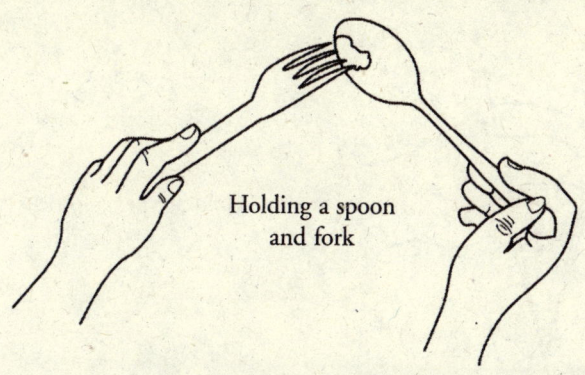
Holding a spoon and fork

4. While using a fork, hold the upper part of the handle between the index and middle fingers just like a spoon, while the thumb holds the fork steady, with the prongs of the fork facing upwards.
5. While using a fork with a knife, the prongs face downwards with the fork held in the left hand.
6. While using a knife, held in the right hand, cover the end of the knife with your palm, resting the index finger about an inch down the handle to help you press down firmly.
7. Avoid cutting the entire portion of the food into small pieces before eating. Cut one piece at a time. Eat this piece before cutting the other one.
8. You can also use the width of the knife blade to push food onto the back of the fork.
9. Do not forget to teach your child the use of a spoon, fork and knife.
10. Once you pick up a piece of cutlery, it should not touch the table again.

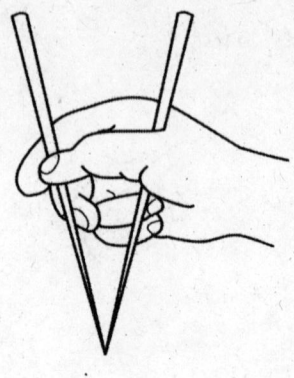

Holding the chopsticks

First chopstick in the web of your right hand

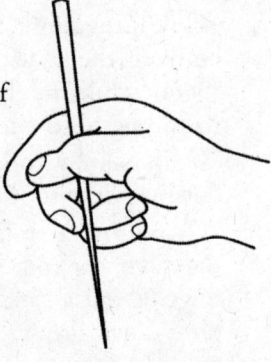

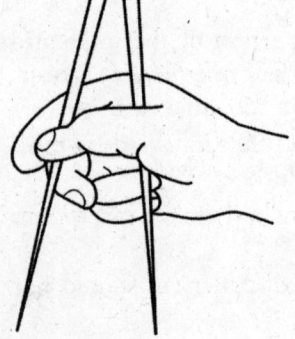

Second chopstick between thumb and index finger

11. Never wave your cutlery in the air to emphasise a point.
12. While using chopsticks, use the thumb and index finger to hold both the sticks, with the remaining fingers giving support.
13. Use the thumb to separate the chopsticks at the bottom, with the index finger acting as leverage, pick up the food between the sticks by tightening the grip of the sticks on the food. Then carry the food between the chopsticks into your mouth.

Napkins

1. When you are seated at the table, wait for your host to make the first napkin move.
2. Similarly, it is the host who will be the first to place the napkin on the table to signal that the meal is over.
3. Never 'flap' the napkin to unfold it, but gently open it on your lap.
4. In case you leave the table during the meal, place the napkin on your chair.
5. At the end of the meal do not refold the napkin, but place it loosely on the table to the left of your plate.
6. A napkin can be laid in the centre of a plate or on a side-plate.
7. It can be folded simply, or arranged artistically.
8. It should be freshly laundered, and should look and feel so.
9. You can use the napkin for wiping your hands or dabbing your lips, but never as a face towel.

Plates and Glasses

1. Two plates are normally used for a sit-down lunch or dinner, the bigger one in the centre, and the smaller one (the side-plate) to the left of it.
2. The bigger plate is used for serving the main course, while the side-plate is used for bread, chappati, salad, etc.
3. A small third plate may be placed on the table just above the side-plate, to hold the soup bowl, but this is optional.
4. When you have finished eating you soup, place the spoon on the soup plate.
5. When taking soup, tilt the spoon away from you, and sip from the side and not the front of the spoon.
6. Avoid slurping, making no more noise than a spider.
7. You may tilt the soup bowl away from you to accept the last serving of the soup.
8. Your water glass or goblet should rest at the tip of your knife.
9. In large restaurants and hotels, and formal dinners, wine and champagne glasses are also placed next to the water glass on its right.
10. If wine or champagne is served, after drinking it, place the glass in its original place.
11. When the plates are arranged on the table. The knife is placed on the right of the main plate, with the blade facing the plate, the fork with its prongs facing upwards on the left, and the spoon horizontally across the top.

Champagne Glass

Wine Glass

Water Glass

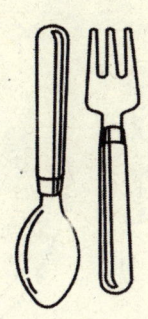

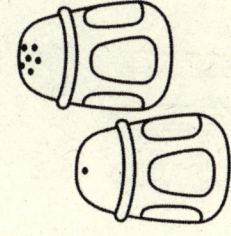

Salt and Pepper

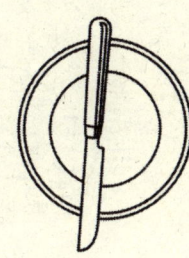

Butter Plate

Formal Setting

Fish Knife
Dinner Knife
Soup Spoon

Napkin
Main Plate

Dinner Fork
Fish Fork
Salad Fork

Dessertspoon and Fork
Water Glass
Dinner Knife
Small Plate
Fork
Salad Knife
Soup Spoon

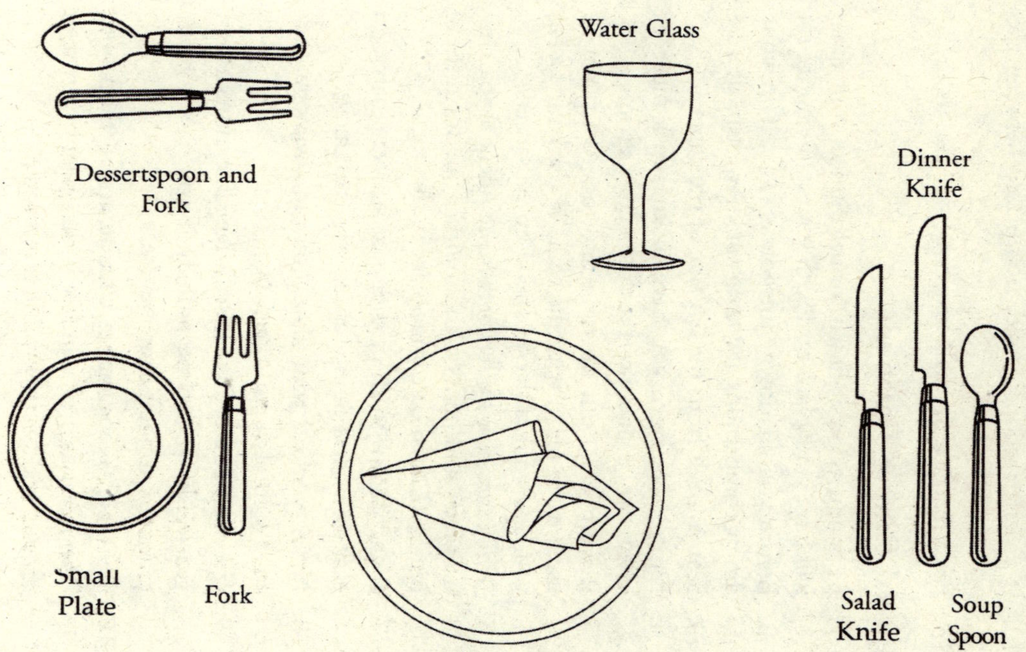

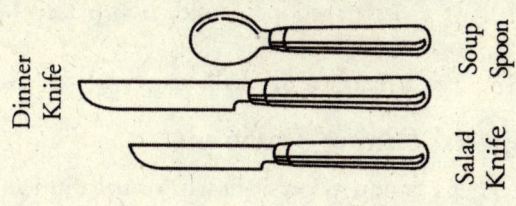

12. If a dessertspoon is used, it is placed between the plate and the knife.
13. For a *thali* meal, small steel bowls are also used.

Special Dining Situations

1. At banquets or sit-down formal dinners your table will have your place card with your name on it.
2. Before you sit down, introduce yourself to your dining companions, if you do not know them already.
3. Seat yourself from the left side of the chair.
4. Ensure that once you have picked up a piece of silverware, it does not touch the table again.
5. Remember to put the knife and fork, when not in use, on the plate, with the blade of the knife facing you, and your coffee/teaspoon in the saucers.
6. While attending buffets, if there is a queue for picking up plates and cutlery, and another one for dishing out food, then take your place in the queue.
7. If any item is in short supply at a private party, go easy on it, and do not ask for replenishment.
8. Never overload your plate. You can always go back for a second or third helping.
9. If someone asks you to join his/her table, either accept graciously or decline politely if you have already promised to join someone else.
10. If you are to eat standing, circulate among the people. The advantage of a buffet is that people can drift around and chat with different people.

11. At formal dinner, when wine is served during the meal, if you do not want it, place your fingertips slightly on the rim of the glass, when the server approaches you.
12. Wine is always poured from the right of the diner.
13. Red wine and brandy glasses are held by the bowl, but white wine and champagne glasses are always held by the stem.
14. Courses are served from the left, and removed from the right.
15. When fish is served, remove the fish bones with thumb and index finger, and place them on the side of the plate.
16. You can use a fish knife (if provided) along with a fork (with prongs down) to eat a fish course.
17. Avoid swirling your coffee around too much. It will only end up getting splashed on the saucer.

Eating Out

1. At the outset, choose a place of your choice for lunch or dinner, considering the quality of its food, the ambience, etc.
2. It is always better to book a table in advance in order to avoid the disappointment of waiting for a table, especially, if it is at the peak hour.
3. Remember to reach the restaurant well in time to claim your table.
4. If for some reason, you cancel your outing, it is courteous to inform the restaurant before the appointed time.

5. If you are a large group of people, then the seniormost person sits at the head of the table, with important guests on either side of him/her.
6. Young children should preferably be seated next to their mother. It becomes easier for them to keep a check on their activities.
7. When the waiter arrives with an order for drinks, courtesy demands that you ask the guests first what they would like to have.
8. When the menu card is presented, you are perfectly at liberty to ask the waiter what a particular item contains, or to explain the meaning of a particular dish.
9. The order is placed by the host or the head of the family, to whom the waiter finally presents the bill.
10. At a formal business lunch or dinner, the first order is placed by the guest of honour.
11. Appetisers, starters and the main meal are ordered simultaneously, while the order for the dessert can be placed at the end of the meal.
12. As a guest, try not to voice your opinion if the food is not up to your standard.
13. If, in between courses, you would like something else, you can tell your host who will inform the waiter.
14. Never discuss about a particular dish being very costly or cheap, but quietly choose with discretion.
15. When the bill is presented to the host, do not even be inquisite to look at it.
16. It is very important to remember to tip the waiter, even if the service charges are included in the bill.

17. Generally, the tip is 5 to 10 per cent of the bill. But if you are going dutch with many others, then the tip should be 5 per cent.
18. On entering a restaurant if you spot someone you know, wave out to that person, or smile. After seating your guests or family, you can walk across to him/her to speak for a couple of minutes.
19. If a friend or acquaintance stops at your table, introduce him to all at your table.
20. Once you have finished eating, you may indicate by gesture to the waiter to fetch your bill.
21. Never allow your children to wander around in the restaurant. Engage them in some conversation so that they do not feel neglected.
22. Always sit from the right of the chair that has been pulled out by the waiter.
23. You may rest your elbows on the table before or after dinner (or lunch).
24. Keep a conversation going.
25. Abstain from conversing on such topics that may make one squeamish or sad.
26. When a dish is not within your reach, or near you, avoid reaching across a person to reach it. Ask your neighbour to pass it to you.
27. When you find a glass or a dish dirty, without creating a fuss, ask the waiter to change it for a clean one.
28. When a food particle gets dislodged in between your teeth, use a tooth pick to remove it, while cupping

your hand over your mouth. But at a formal dinner, visit a cloakroom to dislodge it.

29. If your have dropped a piece of cutlery, discreetly get the waiter to fetch you another, and let the dropped item lie wherever it is till the meal is over.
30. Once the meal is over, place your cutlery in the middle of the plate, side by side, and the napkin loosely beside your plate on the left.
31. If you do want to smoke, light up the cigarette after the coffee is consumed, after seeking permission from the rest of the occupants.
32. Do not forget to thank the waiter and the manager for the excellent meal and service.
33. Never burp loudly, and place your hand on your mouth while 'burping' silently.

Toasting Blunders

1. If you are being toasted, sit there calmly, and thank your host later.
2. If you have to toast, do not read from any paper. Let it be either extempore, or commit it to memory.
3. Do not make your toast long; let it be short and apt.
4. If you are the guest of honour, do toast the host in return, either soon after the host has toasted, or during dessert.
5. Do not tap the rim of your glass to get everyones attention.

6. If you are a teetotaler, make a toast with any other soft drink, for it is the thought that counts.
7. You can toast for more than one person, for example, a whole team or an entire family.
8. Do not pre-empt, but allow the host to be the first one to toast.

Business Etiquette

1. Management now values manners in the workplace as never before.
2. It is vitally important to know what to say, how to dress, how to react in various situations, especially as your keep rising higher in the status.

The Corporate Culture

1. Rank or status gives a business organisation the structure it needs to function effectively.
2. Social and corporate behaviour is more formal in a bank than an advertising agency, whereas the hustle and bustle in a newspaper office makes an advertising office seem severely structured.
3. Basically, behaviour that is grounded in good manner, will allow for discrepancies in corporate etiquette.
4. The basics of corporate etiquette begin with the job interviews.
5. You must remember that the company needs to recruit someone, and they are hoping that you are the person they are looking for.
6. Do dress up well, have a list of the points you want to make, and have a pretty good sense of how to respond – these are also assets.
7. Before you attend the interview, find out everything you can about the company – what the company

does, the size of the company, whether it is a national or an international one, the general reputation, etc.

8. It is always good to dress conservatively for interviews.
9. When you enter the interview room, smile and make eye contact with your interviewer.
10. Wait until you are asked to be seated.
11. Do not fidget or handle things on the desk during the meeting.
12. Listen carefully to what you are being asked, and if a difficult question is posed, pause before answering.
13. At the end of the meeting, thank the interviewer cordially, and follow up with a note.
14. It is imperative to arrive on time.
15. Do not volunteer information you have not been asked for.
16. Always be optimistic. Use positive words like, "I am committed to excellence."
17. Your jewellery and footwear should be unobtrusive and blend well with your outfit.
18. Your portfolio briefcase should be polished and clean. It should not bulge.
19. If you are attending a business appointment, and are given the liberty to remove your jacket or coat, do so, but do not roll up your sleeves.
20. Do not dump your briefcase on the other person's desk. Keep it on your lap or stand it on the floor beside your chair.
21. Complimenting people on their appearance with sincerity is perfectly correct.

22. At the office, though, always compliment a colleague's work and not clothes.
23. If someone compliments you, it is not necessary to reciprocate.
24. Never talk about the designer labels of your clothes. Do ask the other person where he or she got his or her clothes and what they cost.
25. Always thank the other person while accepting a compliment.

Introductions

1. The most essential thing about an introduction is to "just do it", else people around you end up feeling invisible or uncomfortable.
2. Remember to have an eye contact and a smile, while shaking hands with the other person.
3. The person who is being presented or introduced is named last as a business etiquette.
4. Persons of lower rank are introduced to persons of greater authority.
   e.g. "Mr/Ms… (MD), I would like you to meet Mr/Ms… (Junior Sales Executive)."
5. While introducing two people to each other, first look at and speak to the higher authority first, and then look at and speak to the lower authority.
6. While introducing, a little information about those being introduced can be included.
   e.g. "Mr/Ms… (Junior Sales Executive) has been with us for a year now."
7. This little information gives them a point to get the conversation going.

8. Once they start talking, you can discreetly withdraw, in case the situation demands it.
9. At business functions, the host should greet the guests upon their arrival, and make them feel welcome.
10. It is not necessary to introduce a newcomer to everyone. You can introduce him/her to the closest group, by saying his name first, and then naming the other.
11. At a business function, if you are not introduced, you should introduce yourself.
12. If the person introducing has forgotten your name, you should smile and offer to shake hands with the nearest person, and say, "I am…"
13. It is just as important on how you make an introduction as how you respond to being introduced by others.
14. The best way to respond to an informal introduction is by saying, "Hello," and can add a bit of information such as, "I saw you on a CNN programme yesterday."
15. In a formal introduction, it is always correct to say, "How do you do Mr/Ms…?
16. In a formal introduction, do not use the person's first name unless he invites you to do so.
17. Everyone should stand up when being introduced.
18. When newcomers arrive at a very large function, only those seated near them will greet them.
19. If for some reason, like being wedged behind the table, you cannot rise, at least lean forward, or rise slightly so as not to appear rude.

20. When someone visits you at the office, rise and come out from behind your desk to welcome the person, unless he is a co-worker, or someone who frequents you.
21. When a senior officer visits his junior frequently the junior should stop what he is doing and give full attention to his senior, even if he remains seated.
22. In a business world, a handshake is the only appropriate physical contact for both men and women; otherwise fold your hands together in a 'namaskar', depending on the type of set-up at the office.
23. The proper handshake is firm but painless, lasts for only three seconds, takes only two or three 'shakes', and is complemented with an eye contact.
24. Keep your fingers together, and your thumb up.
25. More the web of your hand all the way to the web of the other person's hand.
26. Never offer only your fingertips. That is a weak handshake.
27. You shake hands when someone offers his/her hands to you, when meeting someone for the first time, while greeting guests or your host/hostess, when saying goodbye, or renewing an acquaintance.
28. It is not business etiquette to hug or kiss someone, pat on one's back, put your arm around someone, or put your hand on their shoulder.
29. It is a serious business etiquette faux pas to mispronounce someone's name. If you miss it, or are in doubt, ask for it to be repeated in an apologetic manner.

30. If you have a name that is difficult to pronounce, you can help the person, by smiling and saying, "It is a tough name, isn't it?" Then pronounce it plainly without making the other person uncomfortable.
31. It is quite likely that you may remember someone by his face, and forget his name. In such a situation, you can say something like, "Please tell me your name again. I'm having a temporary memory lapse," or "I remember we met at Mr Seth's house a week ago, but I didn't quite catch your name."
32. When you are in the company of people outside your firm, show your boss respect by addressing him as 'Mr/Ms', or 'Sir/Ma'am'.
33. It is appropriate to address a woman in business as 'Ms', unless she specifically wants to be addressed as 'Mrs' or 'Miss'.
34. Never lower one's rank by forgetting titles like 'Senior Vice President' or 'Chief Executive officer'.

Etiquette at Workplace

1. Proper etiquette at the workplace generates efficiency.
2. Establish cordial and respectful relations with your staff, without being bossy.
3. When you are introducing your staff to someone, use their full name.
4. Generally, you never ask your secretary to do some work that you yourself would shun.
5. Do not use the first name of your seniors unless you are specifically invited to do so.

6. When you are visiting someone at the office after fixing up an appointment, do not be late, and if you do arrive late, apologise and explain.
7. Present your card when you tell the receptionist your name and work.
8. Do not remain standing if your host is sitting.
9. Leave at once after the meeting is over.
10. Send a 'Thank-you' within 24 hours of the meeting. Here is an example:

Dear Ram,

The tips that you gave me about how to handle the staff in the present situation were very helpful to me.

Thank you for making time for our meeting and for giving me the tips.

Sincerely,
Madhav

11. If you reach a door first, regardless of gender, you should open it, go through it, and then hold it to make sure that it does not hit the person following.
12. If a senior executive is present, allow him/her to reach the door and go through it first.
13. If you see someone laden with things, regardless of gender or status, hold the door for him.
14. If you are the host, open the door for your guest and motion them to go in first.
15. Always thank the person who holds the door for you.
16. When you use a lift, if you get into it first, hold the door until all have entered.

17. If you happen to be near the control panel, ask the others what floor they need, and press the button, accordingly.
18. Smoking, once considered sophisticated, is now known to be offensive and dangerous. Hence always seek the permission of those around you before lighting up.
19. It is quite acceptable to politely tell someone to stop smoking in your presence, or to smoke elsewhere.
20. When you do not see an ash-tray, do not smoke.
21. When you speak to someone on the telephone, what you say, how you say it, and the tone of your voice are very important in creating your first impression.
22. When you speak on the telephone, speak clearly, but not too loudly.
23. Avoid chewing, eating or drinking while speaking on the telephone.
24. Try to receive the phone as soon as you hear it ringing.
25. Always identify yourself, with both your name and company or department.
26. Place your calls whenever possible.
27. When a person at the other end is asked to wait while you finish speaking to someone on the other line, make sure that you do not keep him waiting for too long, or politely tell him that you will call him shortly as you are busy on the other line.
28. Every business call should begin with the caller introducing himself, identifying his company, and informing about the who the call is intended for, thus saving the time.

29. Try to place your calls when it is convenient for the other person, not when it is a rush hour for either of you or when the person is just about to leave office.
30. If your call gets disconnected, your must promptly call back, whatever the circumstance.
31. The way you end a call is always remembered by the other person. Always try to end on a positive note.
32. During business calls, never say "see ya", or "Later", just say "Goodbye", and allow the other person to hang up before replacing the receiver.
33. If the other person is wasting your time with useless talk, politely excuse yourself stressing on your busy schedule, and that you will get in touch with him at a more leisurely hour.
34. When you are not able to reach a particular person after repeated tries, it is always a bonus to get to know the person's secretary's name. Addressing the secretary by name scores a lot of points, like gaining confidence and courtesy (the secretary normally acts as a gatekeeper and by his/her becoming your ally, you can reach the boss quicker).
35. The voice mail is a very good and useful tool for conveying information within your company.
36. The message on the voice mail should include the journalist's five Ws— who, what, when, where and why.
e.g. This is Anand on Monday, August 1. I will be out all day and hope to return by 9 pm. Please leave your name, telephone number and a brief message.
37. Before recording your voice on an answering machine, be specific and brief.

e.g. This is Badri speaking. At the sound of a beep, please leave your name, telephone number and the best time to reach you. I will return your call as soon as possible.

38. If you are answering, then give your full name, the reason for your call, the best time you can be reached and your complete telephone number.
39. When you organise a board meeting, be cordial and formal towards the board members.
40. Always arrive on time at the meeting, and do not dash back to your office before the meeting has ended.
41. Offer to help the head of the organisation with access to special information or contacts.
42. Ensure that everything is in place, and nothing is missing.
43. Always thank the volunteer who organised the meeting.

Boardroom Etiquette

1. Before attending the meeting, read all the material provided, in advance, including the agenda, who all will be attending, etc.
2. Never be late (or too early) for others have taken the trouble to be punctual.
3. Ensure that you have all the things required for the meeting — agenda, stationery, etc.— at hand to avoid searching for them during the meeting.
4. Place your briefcases and purses on the floor, not on a chair nearby or the conference table.
5. Avoid doodling on your notepad, or fidgeting with clips or pens (especially if they are jotter pens that

you click to open or close. The clicking sound can be quite annoying!

6. Avoid crossing your legs (though you may cross it at the ankles) as it gives the impression of casusalness.
7. Be formally attired. Make sure that your shoes are polished.
8. Avoid crossing your arms, which according to body language, spells hostility or aggression.
9. Do not slouch, but sit straight. Be attentive and alert.
10. When you enter the room, shake hands with your colleagues, and introduce yourself to those who do not know you.
11. Think before you speak. Speak briefly and to the point.
12. It is wiser to be circumspect, than establishing battle lines.

e.g. Say, "I would like to disagree because it seems to me that…" instead of, "You are wrong. If you had read the document, you would know by now that…"

13. Avoid interrupting someone who is speaking. Wait for the person to complete what he/she is saying before speaking.
14. It is better to make suggestions and recommendations rather than to give orders or take an adamant stance.
15. Speak positively and use "we" when referring to your company, etc.
16. Use honorifics, even though you may be on a first name basis, saying, "Mr Ramprasad says that…" instead of "Sanjay says that…"
17. If you are going to chair the meeting, see that the meeting time is convenient for all, avoiding Monday

mornings and Friday afternoons (if it is a 5-day week, else avoid Saturday afternoons)
18. The two seats on either side of the Chairman should be reserved for the two most important people attending a meeting.
19. Keep the atmosphere conducive for a frank and open discussion, and mediate during conflictual situations to cease the tension.
20. Provide breaks for people to use the toilets or make telephone calls.
21. At the end of the meeting, do not forget to give credit to the deserving and thank everyone for attending the meeting.
22. If name tags are provided, they should bear the first and last names, without the Mr, Mrs or Ms.
23. Make sure that each person has within his/her reach a glass and bottled water; you can add some eats too, provided it is nothing very heavy and greasy.
24. The agenda must include all items that are to be discussed, with time specifications.
25. A copy of the agenda must be distributed to all members well in advance of the meeting.

Business Meals

1. Your social skills and business acumen are evident by your ability to plan and organise, and your level of sophication.
2. Always study the situation from the host's point of view to make you a more confident and knowledgeable guest.

3. The host must ensure that everyone's focus is on the meal, and that nothing distracts its smooth functioning.
4. It is wise not to experiment, but frequent some good restaurants and become familiar with the menu and the maitre d'.
5. Avoid extravagance. Pick a quality restaurant noted for its good and reliable services.
6. Book a table that is in a quiet corner where business can be discussed without too many noisy disturbances.
7. Arrive at the restaurant well before the guests.
8. Leave instructions at the counter to usher in your guests to your table.
9. You need to stand up when your guests arrive, and wait for them to be seated before you resume your seat.
10. Once seated, unfold your napkin on your lap.
11. If the server comes with an order for drinks, ask your guest what they would like, and if they decline, you too must do so.
12. If you do not take alcohol, you can order a soft drink for yourself.
13. After the first round of drinks, ask your guest if they would like another, and if they decline, ask the server for the menu card, and ask your guests what they would like.
14. At the end of the meal, encourage your guest to have dessert, and later tea or coffee.
15. Settle the bill quietly, without fiddling around with small bills or change.

16. You have every right to check the bill, and if there is any discrepancy, deal with it after your guests have left.
17. Never bring out your calculator at the table.
18. Remember to tip the waiter generously.
19. Escort your guests to the door, shake hands with them, and thank them for their valuable time.
20. Once your guests have departed, thank the maitre d'.

Business Card

1. Your business card is an important and personal part of your interaction within the corporate circle, you should know how and when to use it.
2. Your card should comprise your name, company, designation, phone and fax numbers and email address.
3. You can send your card clipped with a document, photograph, magazine, etc., to someone who will find the information useful.
4. You can send it with a gift or flowers.
5. When you present a card to someone, see that the printed side faces up.
6. When someone gives you his card, look at him first and then at the card to establish a connection.
7. Be selective about whom you wish to present your card.
8. Avoid handing out soiled business cards.
9. Always carry a few cards with you. You never know when you may need them.

Etiquette for Occasions

1. If your guest leave with the overall impression of having been warmly welcomed by gracious people, and of having had a fine time, then you have entertained well.
2. What matters most, apart from exuding warmth, is to have everything neat and clean.
3. You do not have to make purchases with whatever you have.
4. If you are not good in cooking, and are not confident about providing a good meal, opt for a catering restaurant, that will supply a good meal.
5. When you feel that you cannot handle the party all alone, you can rope in a friend who would be willing to help you out.
6. You can host a party where you can bring together people who do not know each other but who will probably enjoy meeting one another.
7. Sometimes, it is nice to have old friends together who never seem to get an opportunity to be together.
8. Do not invite someone who you consider will not fit into the group of invitees.
9. Try to always include a person who loves to talk, can be a good conversationist, and will amuse a handful of people and get others talking as well.
10. When an unexpected guest drops by, try to accommodate him/her in a graceful and cheerful manner.

11. You can invite your guests by telephone, saving you time, and getting a quick response.
12. Make your voice welcoming and inviting, and give details about who all are being invited, the date of the party and the reason for it.
13. When you are accepting an invitation, respond before asking who else will be present at the party.
14. If you are getting food catered for the party, you can opt for those who also supply plates, cutlery, etc., with the food, or else use your own crockery and just order for the food.
15. If you include drinks, ensure that the drinks session gets over well in time for dinner.
16. While purchasing the drinks, you do not need to be extravagant and elegant, but be generous and see that there is enough.
17. Where drinks are served chilled, ensure that they are bought well in advance to have them chilled.
18. It is the hosts duty to make sure the glasses are replenished.

Party Time for Adults

1. Generally speaking, a party is a good time to relax and meet everyone.
2. You need not have any reason for having a party, though birthdays, anniversaries and engagements are good enough reasons.
3. Regarding your mix of guests, it is good to combine some familiar faces with new ones.
4. Avoid shop talk that may exclude other guests, and try including everyone in the conversation.

5. Try to have a mix of non-stop talkers with silent ones, so that you eliminate a cacophony of noises from all corners of the room.
6. Courtesy demands that you send a written invitation to the invitees, unless you are very close to the person.
7. If you have accepted the invitation for the party, and are unable to attend it at the last moment, ring up and apologise to your host.
8. Cook food that is simple, tested and tasty.
9. Let there be some variety so that people have a choice.
10. If you are serving non-vegetarian fare, be sure to include vegetarian items for those who abstain from eating non-vegetarian dishes.
11. As the host or hostess, make sure that you welcome each guest individually, dividing your time equally between them, ensuring they are all being served food and drinks, and that they are at ease.
12. Arriving very late at a party is unforgivable, so arrive well in time to join the others.
13. If you have a guest staying with you, it would be uncivil to take him/her along to the party without letting your host know well in advance.
14. It is always good to leave at a reasonable hour.
15. Be profuse in your thanks to your host. Compliment him/her on their choice of food, décor, etc.

Children's Party

1. Always remember that children, are very energetic, and so like to have a lot of entertainment and amusement.
2. The occasion can be a birthday, a naming ceremony, the birth of a baby, or just about anything.

3. Children normally like to give and receive presents, so ensure that if your child receives presents from others, he or she gives them something in return.
4. The guests should include the neighbourhood kids also. Include even those with whom your child is not very friendly, so that the other child does not feel hurt and left out.
5. The invitees can be invited either verbally or by sending them the readily available special printed invitation cards.
6. It is always good to let the parents of the children know when the party is likely to begin and end, so that they can arrange to take them home.
7. For the children's party, punctuality should be observed. Otherwise your child might miss some of the recreational games that have been arranged for them.
8. Ensure that you have a reward for each game that is played.
9. After the cake is cut (or, whatever the occasion, when it ends), see that the children have their plates filled and that each one has a place to sit.
10. If your child is a guest, make sure that he/she thanks the friends and their parents before taking leave of them.

Office Parties

1. Since seniors and juniors get together at office parties. Usually juniors are hesitant in mixing with their peers. Make sure everyone is at ease, and intermingle freely.

2. The host should welcome everyone individually.
3. Punctuality is a must in such parties. Women should, be businesslike at such parties, though they may move and talk freely amongst their male colleagues.
4. Be careful that no one gets inebriated and makes a nuisance of himself.

Deaths and Funerals

1. When tragedy strikes a near one, the most important chore is to inform all the relatives, friends and colleagues and all those who were close to him/her.
2. Offer whatever help you can to the bereaved family.
3. Offer your condolences to all those affected by the death of their near ones.
4. You may not be able to express your grief to them, but try to speak from your heart which will have a genuine ring to it.
5. You can carry some flowers or a garland or a wreath that you can place over the body.
6. Avoid wearing bright-coloured clothes, heavy make-up and jewellery. Sober clothes, preferably, in white, black, or some pastel shade would do.
7. Try to avoid taking children to funerals as they may not know the seriousness of the occasion.
8. If you are in a distant place, send a letter of heartfelt condolence at once.
9. Always acknowledge all letters of condolence at an appropriate time.

Saying the Right Thing

Stereotypes

1. The basic foundation stone of etiquette is one of kindness and respect for others.
2. Set aside all preconceived ideas about correct behaviour, and tackle any new situation with an open and inquiring mind.
3. If you are visiting another country and are hosting a party for people from different cultures, do not hesitate to confess your ignorance about the etiquette, and ask for help.
4. Do not generalise that visitors from abroad are to be taken to an ethnic restaurant, serving what you consider the visitors favourite food.
5. Jettison the notions that Asians are remote, Japanese are basically shy, Germans are cold and super-efficient, etc.

Greetings

1. The styles and methods of greeting varies greatly around the world.
2. Just remember that the moment of greeting is crucial. It is then that the first impression is made.
3. Most Asians, especially the Japanese, customarily bow their head slightly as a greeting gesture, though they have learned to accept the handshake while dealing with westerners.

4. Indians join their hands together, palms together, in front of their chest, and bow slightly when greeting someone.
5. Amongst the Latinos, they greet each other with a slight embrace.
6. The Muslim males hug each other, but avoid contact with the females, just touching their fingers to their forehead as a greeting.
7. The people of countries like France, Spain, Italy and Portugal greet friends by kissing on both cheeks.
8. Americans and British shake hands, with a smile sending out a friendly signal – the same smile may be construed as 'Excuse me' or 'Please' in some Latin Cultures.
9. Many cultures do not encourage eye contact while greeting, as a mark of respect. This could lead to a lot of misunderstanding unless one is familiar with the manner of greeting of that particular culture.

Business Dealings

1. American business people are considered very open and friendly. Foreigners however find this friendliness short-lived.
2. Business people from other cultures are put off by the abruptness of the Americans, for whom time is money.
3. Most Asians and Middle Easterners do not think much of the American attitude of 'Let's get right down to business'.
4. Americans, being friendly, tend to jump onto first-name terms rather quickly which is wrong.

5. In high-context countries like Greece, Spain, Turkey, China, Japan, Korea, Latin America and the Arab World, there is more emphasis on non-verbal communication, indirect verbal signals and implicit meanings. Rituals are important, and time is not the focus.
6. In countries like the United States, Canada, Germany, Switzerland, and the Scandinavian countries, the focus is on a lot of specificity, clear descriptions and unambiguity.
7. When dealing with people, patience pays, and it is good to remember that a lot of things are happening at once.

e.g. An American arrives on time for his meeting with his Korean counterpart, though he expects to be kept waiting. He waits quietly, and when the host does appear, they shake hands, and the American bows his head slightly. The others in the room are introduced to him, and he greets them with more handshakes and slight bows. He partakes of the refreshments if they are served. All the while, his host is hospitable and gracious to which the American responds likewise. Neither of them discuss business. The host may hold several conversations at once, talk on the telephone, veer off the subject, return to the important issue, but ultimately, things will get done, and everyone will take leave of the host in a cordial manner. The American will consider such business tactics as inefficient, but this works for a large section of the world.

Gifts

1. In some Asian cultures like Japanese and Chinese, gifts are not opened in the presence of the guest.
2. Since the Japanese do not consider white or black paper wrappings as a good omen, use wrappings of any other colour, preferably in pastel shades and without a bow.
3. The Chinese consider white flowers a symbol of mourning.
4. For some Latinos and Middle Easterners, yellow flowers denote negative connotations.
5. Red roses signal romantic intent for the Europeans.
6. Chrysanthemums in Europe are linked with death.
7. Gifts that depict partially clad women or pets are not welcome in the Middle East.
8. Make sure that when you present cash gifts to the Chinese, they are in even numbers, and given with both hands.
9. Latinos consider gifts of knives as a 'cutting' of a relationship.
10. Avoid giving four of anything to a Korean or a Japanese.
11. Do not gift a clock to a Chinese.
12. A handkerchief is considered an inappropriate gift in the Middle East, for it denotes tears or parting.

When to Eat

1. Most American executives like to conduct their business at breakfast.
2. They like to have their water glasses filled with ice and drink decaffeinated coffee.

3. While in most countries the main meal of the day is taken at midday, in America it is at the end of the work day.
4. While the main meal is generally taken around 7 pm in America, in Spain, it commonly begins at 10 pm.
5. The English 'tea' is usually around 4 pm, served with sandwiches, or pastries, or tarts.
6. A foreigner will probably find the timing of the American 'brunch' rather disconcerting.

Varieties of 'Strange' Foods

1. Many foreigners find American food like hot dogs, crawfish, marshmallows, sweet potatoes, grits and pumpkin pie, unusual, or, in some cases, repulsive.
2. Many Americans and Englishmen may have the same reaction to things like sea slugs in China, sea urchins in Korea, sheep's eyes in the Middle East, sheep's organs and entrails in Scotland, horse meat in Japan, or toasted grasshoppers in Mexico.
3. When you are in a foreign country and confronted with unfamiliar food, and you do not know what it is, either taste it or refuse politely. If you are asked for your opinion, say something tactful like, "It has a distinctive flavour!"
4. Respect the sentiments of people you are dining with, and avoid eating something that offends their sensitivities.
5. Muslims do not eat the flesh of scavenging animals like pigs, certain birds and lobsters, though their products, such as oil, are used.

6. Muslims do not drink alcohol. Food cooked with alcohol are also taboo for them.
7. When eating with Chinese, ensure that you do not point with your chopsticks or suck on them.
8. Avoid sticking chopsticks upright in your rice, as this denotes the onset of bad luck.
9. Orthodox Jews eat meat and fowl that are ritually slaughtered, and they abstain from pork or shellfish.
10. Formal Chinese banquets, have many courses.

Talking Distance

1. Asians usually maintain some distance from their guests while conversing, unlike the Americans.
2. People in the Mediterranean and Latin countries stand so close that most people feel that their 'space' is being violated, and involuntarily step back.
3. Do not touch the arm or hand of an Asian while you are talking with one. An Asian usually resents being touched.

Gestures

1. Avoid beckoning someone using the crooked index finger.
2. Do not clap or snap your fingers to get the attention of waiters or servants.
3. While in England, do not use the 'V for victory' sign with the palm turned inward.
4. Do not prop up your foot so that the sole of your shoe is facing your guest, especially in most Asian and Middle East countries.

5. It is considered rude in some cultures to stand with arms folded over the chest or with your hands on your hips while conversing.

Giving Criticism

1. Whenever you are criticising a person for some error or blunder, you can soften the attack by being circumspect and tactful.

e.g. Do not say, "You are wrong. How did you arrive at such a figure?" Instead, you could say, "I am getting a different answer. Shall we check it together?"

2. It is always good to involve the other person by using 'we' instead of 'I' as in the above example.

3. If someone criticises you, you will tend to become defensive, but your response should be given with equanimity.

e.g. You can say, "I think you have been misinformed," or "Is that so; let us have a look at this then, "or "that doesn't sound quite right to me."

4. Avoid using the word 'but' which immediately sends up a flare and triggers a defensive reaction.

e.g. "Your speech was very well delivered, but…" Instead, say something like, "Your speech was very well delivered, and next time I suggest you also include…"

5. When criticising, talk about behaviour, and not personality.

e.g. Never say some act was 'wrong' or 'stupid'.

6. Let your comments be in private, and not before a crowd which the person concerned might find humiliating.

7. Be very specific in your comments.

8. Soften the impact of your criticism by beginning with a compliment.

e.g. You are such a gentle person; that is why I was surprised when you raised your voice against them.

9. Sometimes it is wiser to criticise in the form of an advice.

e.g. Instead of saying, "You will never improve your handwriting if you keep scrawling," you could say, "Try to form your letters legibly and write slowly."

Receiving Criticisms

1. If there is any justification in a criticism, accept it gracefully, and make it clear that you will settle the problem.
2. If the criticism is unjustified, do not fly off the handle that will make you regret later. Put off the discussion by saying, "Let's talk about this when we are both calmer, "or, "Let us get together some time and sort this out."
3. If someone is very critical of you in the presence of others, you can stop whatever you are doing or saying, and look him in the eye for a moment, thus 'freezing' him, or say something like, 'Please tell me your views in private."
4. When you are unsure of the validity of the criticism, you can stall by saying, "I will need to think about it, and I will get back to you."
5. If you have erred or goofed, it is best to apologise and say, "I never intended to…, and I am sorry to have offended you."
6. It is never good to insult people, but if you have to do it, do so with grace and style.

7. A compliment benefits both the giver and the receiver.
8. While complimenting, be sincere, otherwise it instantly destroys your credibility.
9. Be specific.
e.g. "The pudding was excellent," instead of "You cook well."
10. Do not make the mistake of giving unqualified praise.
e.g. "That was a good meal, considering…"
11. Do not disagree when a person is complimenting you. Just smile and say "thank you."
12. When someone compliments you on a good job, do not say, "It was nothing," for this is insulting to the other person, denoting that his/her standards are wanting.
13. Do not unilaterally add more merit to a compliment.
e.g. If someone says, "The meal was good," do not add, "Good? It was excellent… everyone lapped it up!"
14. When a compliment has to be shared do not fail to mention that the others also deserve the credit, and acknowledge the credit.

Delivering Bad News

1. If some calamity befalls someone you know, acknowledge the misfortune at the earliest opportunity.
2. If you are attending a funeral, offer your condolences, by simply saying, "I'm very sorry about your loss," or simply, "I'm sorry."
3. When someone is giving you bad news and giving you details about it, remain silent and listen to him attentively, and at the appropriate time you can say

something soothing like, "It must be a taxing period for you, I am sorry."

4. Do not relate another similar incident, where the other person is suffering even more, for that gives the impression of one-upmanship, making him/her feel worse.
5. Remember that it is no time for unsolicited advice.
6. Do not pry into the other person's trouble. Let him volunteer to tell you whatever he wants you to know.
7. You can share in your colleague's grief at the work arena which may be fraught with difficult situations, by assuring your colleague that he/she is not alone, and you stand by him.
8. Never say, "I told you such a thing would happen," or "Everything will work out for the best." Instead, you could say, "I'm sorry you have to go through this," or "Is there anything I can do to help?"
9. If you are sexually harassed, it is best to deal with the abuser by pricking his/her ego, by saying something like, "I'm sure you don't think that was sexually attractive. In fact, it was so comical! You are truly making a fool of yourself!" or "You were pathetic, you silly man/woman," or "I am going to forget this happened, but if you repeat this, believe me, you are going to be in more trouble than you can imagine."
10. If you are in an embarrassing situation, where someone's fly is open, the sari has stepped down off the shoulder, or someone has bad breath, you can directly, but discreetly, say to the person out of earshot of other people, "Your fly is open," "Your *pallau* has fallen away," or "I think you need to gargle your mouth with a mouth wash."

11. If you do not know the person, directly find someone who can convey the message.
12. Never ever ask the following inappropriate questions:
    "How much money do you make?"
    "How come you do not have any children?"
    "Are you two sleeping together?"
13. If someone does ask you such a question, your favourite tactic should be, "Why do you ask?"
14. When someone is going to repeat an often repeated story, you can say, "Oh, that story about your losing your spectacles? Well, that is really hilarious!" and jump in with a new topic of conversation.
15. When someone is verbally attacking your friend who is not there, you can cut short that criticism by saying, "I am sure he/she has a different story to tell. Let us not go into it now."
16. When someone is cracking some vulgar jokes, you can discreetly move away, saying, "I don't think I want to hear this."
17. Have a sense of self-worth and a respect for others which will help you accept criticism without rancor, and deal with conflict without being cowed down by it.

Delivering a Speech

1. When you step on to the dais to deliver a speech, and feel very nervous about it, just remember that the audience is on your side, and that they want you to be as relaxed as they are.
2. Since the stage freight involves the right-side of the brain to function, counter it with some function of the left-side, such as counting or working some problems in your head.

3. Breathe, inhaling through the nose, and exhaling through the mouth.
4. Do not forget to smile — you will feel the tension melting away.
5. Get ready for your talk, ensuring that everything has been prepared in advance — how you want your audience to perceive you, your gestures and voice modulations, whether you want to welcome, motivate, instruct the audience, or explain some situation, or extol a person, a company, etc.
6. Speak while standing, whenever possible.
7. Adjust your talk according to the interests of the audience and sprinkle your talk with humorous anecdotes.
8. Try to be at par with the audience level, without sounding snobbish or self-bragging or hostile.
9. Remember that the audience would like to hear you present the speech or information, rather than just read it from a paper.
10. Be specific about the points you make.
11. Speak clearly and with feeling and enthusiasm.
12. Control your voice — a first-timer will tend to speak loudly or shout due to nervousness.
13. Speak slowly, so that people can follow what you are stating.
14. Avoid rambling and repeating.
15. Keep your talk brief and to the point.
16. When you have finished, say, "Thank you," and sit down.
17. Since first impressions are so vital, open your address by complimenting the audience, or making some provocative or shocking statement, or narrating a joke, etc.

18. Since the last impressions too are of significance, do not be afraid to employ some dramatic or emotional language, or use some lines of stirring poetry or ghazal.
19. If you are introducing a speaker on the podium to the audience, make it brief, and leave yourself out of it as much as possible.

Making Small Talk

1. First size up the person with whom you are going to converse.
2. Smile, make eye contact and shake hands.
3. Introduce yourself, and listen carefully to the other person's name.
4. Repeat the other person's name so that you will not easily forget it.
5. You may start the conversation by saying something about yourself, your work, your family, etc.
6. You need not hesitate to confess that you are a shy person —"Big parties like this intimidate me," or "I like to meet new people, but shyness keeps me from making the first overtures."

Keeping the Conversation Going

1. Learn to lend your ears, and listen to the person speaking patiently, without butting in every now and then.
2. Keep eye contact so that the person knows that your attention is focussed on what he is saying.
3. Try to ask open-ended questions that will keep the conversation going.

e.g. "Why did you come to this decision?" or "How did you manage to escape?" instead of "Did you escape?" which might only have an answer in "Yes" or "No".

4. People like to be asked their opinion concerning major events.

e.g. "The twin towers of World Trade Centre were bombed. Do you think Osama Bin Laden had a hand is this?"

5. Try to change the topic, if it gets boring, in a discreet manner.

e.g. "Talking of bombing, ... what is your opinion about the Taliban?"

6. Do not rush through your conversation. This shows you are anxious that you might not get a chance to give your opinion.
7. Do not talk very slowly and with too may pauses, leaving the other person to finish sentences for you.
8. You have every right to disagree about something – only do not let it drift into a squabble!

Slipping Away

1. It is important that you close the conversation gracefully.
2. Each one of us like people to acknowledge our presence.

e.g. When you are standing with someone at the store, if the shopkeeper looks at you and nods his head, or says "I'll be right with you," the waiting can be less annoying.

3. It is equally aggravating when people just drift away while the conversation is going on, without some acknowledgement that a conversation has occurred.

e.g. You can say, "It was nice talking to you. We shall meet again, I hope."

4. If you do have to move away, wait for a break in the conversation, then say, "Well, I have to say hello to our chief guest. Can we carry on this discussion some other time?"
5. If, for some reason, it is not possible to end the conversation properly, make some sort of parting gesture, like an eye contact and a wave.

Giving and Receiving Gifts

1. It is very important that you give and receive gifts graciously.
2. You must remember that it is the thought that counts, not the worth of the gift.
3. If you receive a gift with an expression of gratitude, the giver will appreciate it very much for he/she has spent time and thought on the selection of the gift.
4. Joke gifts may evoke laughter at that moment, but can leave a sour taste.
5. By nicely wrapping a gift and giving it on time you enhance the value of the gift and your gesture.
6. Watch out what you gift professionally for what you give sets a precedence which must be matched or exceeded in the future.
7. An employee is under no obligation to give a superior a gift — he/she may do so at his/her discretion, or as a spontaneous act.
8. Receiving a nicely wrapped gift with a personal note inside is one of life's nicest experiences.
9. Even if a person has been thanked verbally, it is always good to follow it up with a 'Thank-you' note.

10. Gifts for babies can include pins, mugs, rattles, clothes, silver or gold objects, dresses, albums, baby blanket, music box, or simple toys.
11. Children would love to receive books, toys, craft kits, educational games, sports items, paints and brushes, and video games.
12. Teenagers love books, clothes, audio and video cassettes, sport equipment, camera, watch, etc.
13. For weddings one can present silverware, art objects, money, glassware or pottery, table lamps or brassware, wall hangings, linen, engraved boxes or jewellery boxes, thermoware, like flasks or casseroles, etc.
14. Generally, for anniversaries, gifts are given only on special anniversaries such as a 25th year anniversary.
15. The most suitable gift for anniversaries would be flowers and bouquets, or a basketful of assorted fruits.
16. The "traditional" and "revised" list of gifts for anniversaries is given below:

First	Paper clock
Second	Cotton / China
Third	Leather / Crystal/ Glass
Fourth	Books / Electrical Appliances
Fifth	Wood/ Clock / Silverware
Sixth	Candy/ Iron/ Wood
Seventh	Copper/ Bronze/ Brass / Desk sets
Eighth	Electrical Appliances / Linen/ Lace
Ninth	Pottery / Leather
Tenth	Tin/ Aluminiums / Diamonds
Eleventh	Steel / Fashion/ Jewellery
Twelfth.	Silk/ Linen / Coloured gems/ Pearls
Thirteenth	Lace / Textiles/ Furs
Fourteenth	Ivory / Gold Jewellery
Fifteenth	Crystal / Watches

Sixteenth	Silverware
Seventeenth	Furniture
Eighteenth	Porcelain
Nineteenth	Bronze
Twentieth	Platinum
Twenty-fifth	Silver
Thirtieth	Pearl / Diamond
Thirty-fifth	Coral / Jade
Fortieth	Ruby
Forty-fifth	Sapphire
Fiftieth	Gold

17. For housewarming occasions, you can gift something useful for the house, like big pottery or vases, a welcome mat, plants, clocks, paintings, curios, etc.
18. For birthdays, you can also give birthstones. The following is a list of birthstones by month:

January	Garnet
February	Amethyst
March	Bloodstone or aquamarine
April	Diamond
May	Emerald
June	Pearl or moonstone
July	Ruby
August	Sardonyx or peridot
September	Sapphire
October	Opal or tourmaline
November	Topaz
December	Turquoise

19. Gifts for traveller must be both practical and portable like, musical tapes, vanity kit, books and magazines, small tote bags, travel alarm clock, a leather passport / ticket holder, etc.
20. While giving a gift to someone, think about what would please the recipient, not you.

Demeanour and Poise

1. Demeanour and poise steer the course of our lifestyle.
2. A good posture denotes your good upbringing.
3. An upright, straight and graceful figure shows character.
4. When you sit down in a chair, do it gracefully, without plonking yourself down.
5. As you sit, ensure that your hands are on your lap, or on the armrests.
6. Keep your legs together, and if you do cross one leg over the other, make sure that you do not shake your leg.
7. While standing, stand tall and erect, and do not slouch.
8. To be at ease, you can stand with your feet a little apart and your hands clasped behind you.
9. Do not stand with hands on your hips which shows aggression.
10. While you are conversing, do not let your attention wander, unless you are the host who is welcoming others too.
11. See that your child sits with a straight back, stands with ease, and walks with a head held high, to ensure a good posture, and a confident demeanour.
12. If you are an impatient person, hide it tactfully, by avoiding pacing up and down, glancing at your watch every few seconds, biting your nails, etc.
13. Avoid making wild and unnecessary gestures.

14. While walking with a woman, walk on the outer side as a protective shield.
15. Your personality, taste and fine sense of aesthetics set you apart from the crowd.
16. The way you conduct yourself at public places shows your upbringing.
17. Always remember that you are known by the company you keep.
18. A charming manner evokes a positive response from others, endearing them to you.
19. The qualities of a charming person are poise, elegance, grace and a pleasing manner.
20. To have class, you need to have modesty, honesty, good manners, politeness, sincerity towards relationships, and humanitarian considerations for fellow beings.
21. Always keep your anger under control; otherwise all your virtues will be overshadowed by it and you will be branded as an unpleasant person.

Managing Relationships

1. Always be gracious in all your dealings with people.
2. Handle all unpleasant and sticky situations with tact and gentleness.
3. Always be helpful and amicable with your friends, for true friendship is everlasting.
4. In matters of monetary help to friends, be extra careful.
5. Never take your friends for granted. Do not be possessive about them or patronise them.
6. Learn to respect the feelings and moods of others.

7. When a person or family moves into a vacant house nearby, you could call on them to establish cordial relations.
8. If someone indulges in gossip, it is best to keep a safe distance from that person.
9. If you value your privacy, and find your neighbour bothering you with frequent visits, you can politely tell him/ her that you will spend a longer time with him/ her later when you have time.
10. Treat your assistants and juniors with candour and friendliness without going overboard. Be careful that you do not become too bossy or snobbish.
11. With servants, you have to be strict without being rude or cruel, being sensitive to their needs and background.
12. It is charitable to give servants things that they need every now and then without grumbling. Ensure that their need is genuine.
13. A teacher should be strict while dealing with students, without being harsh. A teacher should also be patient with them and should not discriminate between students.
14. The students should show respect and deference to their teachers. They should conduct themselves well and ensure that they merit the attention of their teacher.
15. If you are a customer in a shop, treat the shopkeeper with deference, for he is not your servant.
16. Do not unnecessarily waste the shopkeeper's time, by asking him to show you everything and then walk out empty-handed.
17. Do not bargain if you see a signboard suggesting that prices are fixed.

18. As a shopkeeper, always greet your customer with a smile.
19. Attend to your customers promptly, and if there is a big crowd, acknowledge the presence of the person trying to catch your attention with a nod, telling him/her, "Just a minute, I'll attend to you in a minute."
20. The parent-child relationship is very important, and children normally emulate their parents.
21. As a parent, be patient with your child, listen to him/her patiently, and make him/ her feel loved. Inculcate human values right from childhood.
22. Establish a healthy relationship with your children, so that they are able to communicate with you easily.
23. Ensure that you child shows deference to elders, and is always polite with them.
24. If a child throws tantrums, treat with iron gloves, making sure that the child knows that he/she cannot have his/her way.
25. Always encourage your children in all their endeavours.
26. Do not show favouritism amongst your children as this will only lead to an inferiority complex in the others.

Clothes and Accessories

1. Always dress to suit your figure, face and personality.
2. Dress simply, unless it is a party.
3. Be distinct and attractive, without being garish or flamboyant.
4. Avoid dressing skimpily, or in offensively revealing or tight clothes.

5. While children can wear bright clothes, those above forty years look graceful in sober clothes with muted colours.
6. While leather belts with big brass buckles look good on youngsters, older people should have smaller buckles on their belts.
7. Do make sure that your shoes are well polished, and are comfortable to wear.
8. Ladies who wear high-heeled shoes or slippers should feel confident and comfortable enough to wear them.
9. Make sure that your socks and handkerchief are spotlessly clean.
10. Ladies handbags, be they leather or denim or jute, should be spacious enough to hold everything that is required, without overstuffing them.
11. For formal wear, ties and suit are suggested. In informal wear, you can even wear a t-shirt, and slip-on shoes.
12. Perfume should be dabbed on with caution. Do not drench yourself in it.

Etiquette at Work

1. Maintain a balance between lack of good manners and too much formality.
2. Use the formal style of addressing your seniors – using Mr Mrs Ms.
3. In some workplaces people are quite comfortable with their staff members using their first names – check the norm prevailing there before taking this step.

4. Always keep your conversation brief and to the point.
5. Be ware and wary of malicious gossip in the office.
6. If you hear any malicious gossip that involves you, nip it in the bud by confronting the gossip monger, and politely but firmly setting the record straight with him/her.
7. Offer to help your colleague who is in trouble, only if you are sure you can.
8. Once you have helped out someone in dire need, do not go about bragging about it.
9. To maintain perfect harmony with your boss, it is certainly not a sin to flatter him/her and pamper his/her ego, provided it is within limits.
10. Treat all your juniors with grace and respect, and bridge any distance that exists between you, without getting too close to them.
11. While settling disputes between employees, see that you hear the details from both parties before settling it.
12. An office memo should be short, polite and to the point. Avoid flippancy and humour.

Correspondence

1. Correspondence can be personal or business related, formal or casual.
2. How your correspondence looks is as important as what is says.
3. Correspondence should always follow a pattern, addressing different people differently according to rules and conventions.
4. Letters reveal more of ourselves than we care to think.
5. A letter is a powerful medium of communication, that can be more touching and intimate than even a conversation.

The Power of the Pen

1. Plain language is enhanced by simplicity and clarity.
2. Your thoughts and meaning should not be hidden behind jargons and clichés, unfamiliar words and long winding phrases.
3. While writing a personal letter to someone, remember to be candid, making any situation clear, and not indulging in unnecessary details that will produce ennui.

e.g. (a letter cited for its virtues in Etiquette Letter Writer Published in 1875 by J.P. Lippincott and Co. Philadelphia)

To her I very much respect – Mrs Margaret Clark
– Lovely, and oh! That I could write loving, Mrs

Margaret Clark; I pray you let affection excuse presumption.

Having been so happy as to enjoy the sight of your sweet countenance and comely body sometimes, when I had occasion to buy treacle or liquorish (sic) powder at the apothecary's shop.

I am so enamored with you, that I can no more keep close my flaming desire to become your servant. And I am the more bold now to write to your sweet self, because I am now my own man and may match where I please; for my father is taken away, and now I am come into my living. If you think well of this notion?

I shall wait upon you as soon as my new clothes is made and hay harvest is in. Your loving servant till death.

Mr Gabriel Bullock

Here, Mr Bullock's intentions of proposal are made clear, avoiding subjects like health, gossip or weather.

The Structure of a Letter

1. If you have difficulty starting a letter, begin with a bit of good news.

e.g. "You will be glad to hear that…"

2. Or you can refer to the last meeting you had with this person.
3. Avoid opening a letter with an apology for not replying sooner, but you may explain for the delay in a tactful manner.

e.g. "You must be thinking that I have forgotten you, but actually you have been in my thoughts often lately. It is just that there has been a lot going on. Instance…"

4. In the body of the letter, write about what has been happening to you or to those around you, keeping the tone conversational.
5. End formal letters with a "Sincerely" and advance toward familiarity with "Yours truly", "Regards", "Best wishes", "Affectionately", etc.
6. Very informal letters can close with "Miss you" or "Write soon".
7. If you do not have a printed address on the top of your letter paper, you may write it in the upper right corner.
8. The date follows below the address at the upper right corner, or at the bottom left corner.
9. Depending upon to whom (a family member or close friend) the letter is addressed, you can use "Yours affectionately", or "As ever" or "As always" or "All best wishes" or "Yours sincerely" (If you do not know the person very well), or "Gratefully" for letter of thanks, or "Respectfully" if used by the clergy.

>D2, Kapila Apts.
>J.L. Puram,
>Mysore-570012
>Sept. 30, 2001

Dear Mr Sharma,

Thank you very much for your letter dated Sept. 20. It was certainly an interesting letter. We will go ahead with the project as you have suggested, and keep you informed of the progress.

>*Sincerely,*
>Rahul Taneja

10. "To Whom It May Concern" is better than "Dear Madam," or "Dear Sir," which are now outdated, when you are writing to someone whose name you do not know.
11. Before inserting the letter into the envelope fold it. If you fold it twice, fold the bottom third first, then the top third.
12. Do not seal letters if they are hand-delivered, unless they are very personal or confidential.
13. Brief, direct sentences are safer than long winded sentences and phrases and idioms.
14. Remember, it is always "between you and me" and not "between you and I", or "between 4 pm to 5 pm".
15. Avoid using the phrase "I, myself", for "myself" is good enough, and use it only for emphasis.
16. Remember that the speaker "implies" while the listener "infers".
17. When using collective terms, remember to match them with their appropriate verbs.
e.g. "A group of people is (not 'are') arriving."
18. Encourage your children to write. They could start by writing out a 'thank-you' note, instead of sending a pre-printed one.

Writing Different Kinds of Letters

1. While writing 'Thank-you' letters, be sure to thank the person for the particular gift, for the effort and energy put into selecting and purchasing it, and how you are going to find it useful.
2. If you have received money, do not mention the amount in your letter of thanks, but you can say "your generous gift" instead.

3. While sending a letter of condolence, acknowledge what a terrible loss the death is for the bereaved, and that you share their grief.
4. Offer your sincere help in any way that would be beneficial to them.
5. Do not forget to extol the virtues, character and accomplishments of the deceased.
6. Keep the style of the condolence letter formal to a certain degree.
7. Do not forget that the condolence letter is sent to comfort the bereaved, and hence avoid stressing how grief-stricken you are.
8. Congratulatory letters are the easiest and happiest of letters that may be kept in the family for posterity.

Dear Himal,

Congratulations on receiving the full-aided scholarship to the state University of New York at Albany. It is not only a tribute to your hard work and brilliance, but it will give you the opportunity to study in a university of repute, and which has one of the best labs in your field in the world today. All of us here at the college share your joy of this moment with you. We will miss you, and wish you all the best in your studies.

With best wishes
Kaushik

9. When you have apologised to someone in person whom you have offended, it is always good to follow it up with a letter of apology, stating clearly and humbly that you are sorry.

10. When writing letters to people in power, be concise, state your position and the reasons for it, and say whom you represent.
11. While dispatching a letter of complaint to a retailer, business, or government agency, be as unemotional as possible, while putting down the facts emphatically.

Writing Notes

1. Sometimes it is much easier to write a note to someone, expressing your wishes, than to confront the person and say it verbally — here the note can work like magic.
2. While drafting your note, think about who it is meant for — an intimate friend, a person you like, someone you have met recently.
3. Also remember the occasion for penning the note — an anniversary, a chance acquaintance, sharing a joy with someone, etc.
4. There are some perennial easy ways to get started while writing a note.
e.g. "What a … (great trip, grand surprise, warm welcome, etc.)"
"I was thinking (or remembering) …"
"I can't tell you how much…"
"It was so very nice of you to…"
5. A closing to your note should reflect the nature of your relationship with the recipient.
e.g. All my love, Best love, Much love, Love, Fondly, Affectionately, Warmly, Regards (in declining order of intimacy).

6. A personal touch is added when you write the note, instead of typing it.

Your Personal Stationery

1. Even a single-sentence letter can speak volumes about the person sending it, based on the way it looks.
2. A very expensive bond paper letter can be valuable to a friend or relative, but of trivial importance to the person with whom you are seeking a job.
3. A clean paper, crisply folded, and neatly filled with relevant details will speak better in your favour than costly stationery that is carelessly used.
4. The best stationery is made from rag cottons, but for letter writing, bond paper is the best.
5. A formal writing paper can be engraved or plain, and must be used for things like responding to formal invitations, or for condolence letters.
6. For informal and friendly correspondence, you can use light-coloured paper, or a paper which has a light printed or embossed background.
7. For business, your letterhead can carry the logo, name and address, with email, fax, etc. of the company.

Sending Invitations and Replying

1. Nowadays, most formal invitations carry the RSVP fixture, as most people do not reply formally and in writing to invitations.
2. While replying to a formal invitation, write by hand, and in third person, using engraved personal or conservative stationery.

3. While sending a "regret" reply, you can say, "due to a previous engagement…" or "because of absence from city…"
4. Informal invitations are written on personal notepaper or on an informal correspondence card.
5. Though informal, yet they are written in third person, but less structured in form.
6. When replying, if there is a telephone number listed on the invitation, call to state your reply.

Sheela and Mohan Rao

Invite you

To cocktails

On Sunday, June 2nd

6-8 o'clock

221 Green Street

R.S.V.P.
4411697

7. Formal invitations are either handwritten, or printed.

Mr & Mrs Navin Parikh

Request the pleasure of your company

at dinner

on Friday the sixth of May at 8 p.m.

1344, Gandhi Marg, Calicut

Addressing People and Envelopes

1. For women 'Ms' is the correct form of address in the business arena, and widely accepted in the social world.
2. When writing to a known person, sign, using your first name only.

3. Never use a title for yourself while signing.
e.g. Mr Patel or Mrs Mary (you may add in parentheses Miss or Ms if you are a single woman).
4. If your name is unisex, help the reader by including (Ms, Miss, Mrs or Mr to the left of your signature in parentheses.
5. All social envelopes should be addressed, written by hand, or typed.
6. Middle names are not always written out on formal envelopes.
e.g. Instead of writing Kaushik Aruna Kumar, you may write Kaushik A. Kumar.
7. When addressing an envelope to a married couple, the woman's name goes first.
e.g. Mrs Tanuja Kapoor and Mr Shammi Kapoor
8. When both halves of a couple are doctors, the envelope must be addressed as The Doctors Cherian, or Dr Eliza Cherian and Dr Thomas Cherian.
9. If only the husband is a doctor, then the address should read as Dr and Mrs Thomas Cherian, or Dr Thomas Cherian and Mrs Eliza Cherian (the name with the title here goes first).
10. When addressing an envelope to a boy, write 'Master' until the age of eight, and 'Mr' at eighteen.
11. Judges are referred to as "The Honourable'.
12. Ambassadors are referred to as 'His/her Excellency'

Games and Travel

Sportsmanship

1. A good sportsperson plays by the rules.
2. He/she always gives opponents the benefit of doubt.
3. A true sportsperson is concerned about everybody's safety.
4. He/she is gracious in both triumph and defeat.

The Gym

1. It is always necessary to exercise common sense and etiquette at places of exercise.
2. Each participant must be sensitive to the needs of others, and try to minimise distractions and promote safety.
3. Dress sensibly while exercising.
4. Ensure that you do not leave your belongings scattered around.
5. If you see someone waiting to use a particular exerciser, do not jump ahead of the person before you. If you are in a tearing hurry it is better to skip it than 'jump' your turn.
6. If you are using an equipment, do not dally and keep another person waiting for it.
7. Avoid grunting, groaning or moaning as they are distracting and only theatrical.
8. Respect the trainer's expertise and time.

The Pool

1. When the pool is busy, lap swimmers should stay in their lane.
2. If you are not in a group, try to find a lane or area that is not being used by a lap swimmer.
3. The best etiquette in swimming is behaving cautiously.
4. Use the wading area, if you cannot swim.
5. If you see a towel on a chair, it indicates that the chair is reserved.
6. Carry drinking water to the beach if it is a hot day, to prevent dehydration.
7. Never leave any trash behind on the beach.
8. Do not swim out beyond the posted limit.

Etiquette on the Links

1. A level of personal integrity is a must for golf.
2. The golfer himself/herself declares the ball to be out of bounds.
3. He/she has to keep his/her own score and report his/her scores to record his/her handicap.
4. A beginner must have a rule book handy, and must study both the rules and traditions of the game.
5. It is necessary to observe a consistent and companionable code of behaviour.
6. Both men and women players should wear comfortable clothes, and use some kind of hat to shield them from the scorching heat and the sun's glare.
7. It is good manners to keep the game moving along.

8. If a party is right behind you, you may ask them to play through.
9. If a party in front is playing slowly, you can ask them if you can play through.
10. You may help your fellow players to track down lost balls and ensure that you carry extra balls.
11. Do not litter the course, and remember that it is not etiquette to eat or drink anything on the course.
12. While teeing off, there is no gender preference.

Racquet Games

1. While at the tennis court, you can help out or even instruct beginners.
2. If you are not sure of a rule, it is okay to ask others for guidance.
3. Verbal and non-verbal temper tantrums should be avoided on the court.
4. Never make a fuss about errors or bad play.
5. Do not find excuses for a bad game such as the weather, you partner or health, when in fact you were plainly outplayed.
6. Extravagance is bad manners in most situations and particularly in sports.

Skiing, Skating and Boating

1. For skiing, ensure that your clothing is not only warm, but will also resist water and wind.
2. The basic rule of politeness includes staying in your place in the lift line.
3. Hold your skis upright in front of you to avoid whacking your neighbours.

4. Once you reach the top, clear the lift area immediately so as to avoid a traffic snarl up.
5. Regardless of your ability, be sure that you never ski alone, for if you fall, no one knows where you are and so no one can come to get you.
6. Ski only on trails that suit your skiing ability.
7. Remember that the slower skier in front of you always has the right of way.
8. If you come across an injured skier, remove his skis but not his shoes, do not attempt to move him, wait for another person to come along, and then go for help to a ski patrol.
9. While skating, stay to the right and pass on the left.
10. Skate smartly. Wear protective gear and master the basics of moving, stopping and turning.
11. Skate legally. Obey all traffic regulations.
12. Skate alertly by controlling your speed, watching out for road hazards, and avoiding pitfalls.
13. While boating, remember the first rule – the captain or skipper is the boss.
14. Be considerate, avoid complaining, and stay out of the way of those working the vessel.
15. Help out in any way you can.
16. Never smoke below decks, in particular, near the galley stove.
17. If you feel seasick, stay on the deck in the fresh air — do not feel embarrassed, for it is not your fault.
18. Use fresh water sparingly.
19. If you own the boat, make sure that there are lifejackets for all.

Travel Preparations

1. Rule number one for travel is 'Be Prepared'.
2. Make sure that you are well groomed and well dressed, for the way we dress is a symbol of who we are, or what kind of a person we are.
3. If you are travelling overseas, be sure that you have a small amount of local currency at hand.
4. Travel light, ensuring that you do not carry too many clothes and paraphernalia that can be avoided.
5. Carry all necessary documents — passport, visa, driver's licence, medical prescriptions, inoculation records, tickets, ATM and other credit cards, etc.
6. It is always good to draw up an itinerary, and leave a copy of it with someone with whom you hope to be in constant contact.
7. Make use of your travel agent to book all the reservations for the various laps of the journey, car rentals, tour guides, etc.

Hotel Services

1. If you are booking into a luxury hotel, ensure that it is done well in advance.
2. If the doorman hails a cab for you, give him a tip.
3. Tipping a porter or bell-boy is also allowed.
4. When you are shown to your room, make sure that you have the requisite towels, pillows, blankets, hangars, water to drink, etc.
5. If you are travelling on business, place your breakfast order the night before, allowing yourself plenty of time.
6. Be careful that you do not keep cash or valuables in your hotel room.

7. Check out after indicating to the reception your plans well before check-out time.
8. Always leave your room tidy.

Advice for Women Travelling Alone

1. Always make sure you are on an equal footing with men.
2. Do not be afraid to talk to strangers, for they might become the most interesting part of your trip — just be wary of putting yourself in jeopardy.
3. If you are not interested in communicating with someone, just respond by a nod, a smile, or monosyllabic answers.
4. In the dining room, do not be afraid to pull up a manager about discriminatory practices if you think it is warranted, but do so quietly, yet firmly.
5. If you agree to dine with a man, be sure to dine in the hotel dining room, and charge your meal to your room, thus avoiding any miscommunication about the nature of the date.
6. In your room, check your windows and door locks, and ensure that the telephone is in working order.
7. Never admit anyone to your room when you have not invited or requested through the hotel — repairman, plumber — without calling the front desk first.

Airplane Etiquette

1. Do not show up at the airport with arms laden with plastic bags, newspapers, knick-knacks and snacks.
2. Make sure that your luggage tags are secure.
3. Remember that you have to carry your own luggage, either in your hands or in a cart.

4. Keep a watch on your own luggage and do not be quick to agree to watch someone else's luggage — you never know what illegal object could be inside, or you may need to move on.
5. Make sure you do not stand in the aisle longer than necessary, else you will be holding up other passengers who are waiting to go past you.
6. Always wait until all the emergency instructions are announced before you use the earplugs or blindfolds.
7. Reserve an aisle seat if you intend to walk a bit.
8. Do not push the 'call' button unnecessarily.
9. Leave the bathrooms as clean as they were when you entered them.
10. It is polite to ask your neighbour if he/she minds your working on a laptop.
11. Make sure that your telephone calls are kept to an absolute minimum.
12. If a delay means you have to dash to make a connection, tell the flight attendants before landing, so that they can assist you in deboarding quickly.
13. While leaving the plane, do not get into the aisle until you are ready to proceed towards the door.
14. If there is a delay due to a blizzard, a hurricane, a thunderstorm, etc, or you may be provided a reservation on the next possible flight with vouchers for meals and hotel if necessary. Explaining your problem quietly and politely could have a better shot at getting the last seat – if one becomes open – than yelling, threatening and throwing tantrums.
15. When your luggage does not get unloaded after you disembark, report to the airline office for reclaiming the luggage.

16. Always carry your medicines, nightdress, cash, jewellery, toiletries, a change of clothes, etc., in your hand luggage.

Ship Etiquette

1. While booking reservations on a ship, get a diagram of the ship in advance, so you will know where you are staying —the most expensive accommodations are the larger rooms, higher up and on the outside.
2. Pack light as space is limited on the ship.
3. Address the skipper as Captain and the other officers as Mr, Mrs, or Ms.
4. If the captain invites you to a reception, do not monopolise him in conversation.
5. If you are invited to dine at the captain's table — a high honour — be on time, and introduce yourself to your dining partners.
6. You may be seated with strangers. If you are unhappy with the arrangement, you may ask the steward to assign you to another one. Do not request seating at an officer's table (that is considered a bestowed honour).
7. Daytime dress in casual, while dinner is generally formal.

Auto Etiquette

1. If you are driving, do not take chances while driving, for it is disconcerting to the passengers, and can create tensions.
2. Never smoke in another's car.
3. Do not use cellular phone unless it is absolutely necessary.
4. Park in well-lighted areas.

5. Never stop when waved down by someone standing by a "disabled" car, but drive on to the next service station and inform its manager or attendant.
6. Never stop for a hitchhiker.
7. If you re stopped by the police for a driving violation or any other reason, be straightforward and polite, never argumentative.
8. If you are involved in an accident, stay cool, and do not trade accusations with the other driver.
9. If you scrape someone's fender, and they are not in the car, do not bolt away, but leave your name and telephone number under a windshield wiper blade.
10. It is polite to offer an older person or the highest ranking person in the group of the front passenger seat.

Train Etiquette

1. The basic rules of courtesy as used on airplanes are applicable to train travel as well.
2. Bring blindfolds and earplugs for sleeping.
3. If you want to open or close a window, ask the person next to you if he/she minds.
4. Remember not to litter the floor.
5. Smoke only in designated areas.
6. Keep your children from running up and down the aisles.
7. Do not dump your briefcase and other pieces of luggage on the seat.
8. If you are able-bodied, giving up your seat to the elderly or disabled person is still the civil and decent thing to do.

9. Lend a hand to someone who is struggling to heave bags onto an overhead rack.

Bus Etiquette

1. Avoid loud conversations.
2. Give your seat to an elderly person, a disabled one, or a woman with a child in her arms.
3. Do not talk to the driver while the bus is in motion.

Tidbits

1. The use of "Please", "Thank you", "You're welcome", "Excuse me" let people know that you have good manners.
2. Look people in the eye when you speak to them.
3. When you are introduced, stand up and say, "Nice to meet you," or "Hello," or "How do you do?"
4. If your child asks you, "What is the 'worst' thing a person can do?" your answer should be, "To hurt someone's feelings."
5. The most important thing about introductions is to actually make them.
6. Join in a conversation to make a meal more enjoyable.
7. Start eating only when everyone is seated and has been served.
8. If you drop something during a meal at home, pick it up. At a friend's house, leave it until the meal is over, then pick it up.
9. If you have to blow your nose, or dislodge something stuck between your teeth, excuse yourself and leave the table.
10. If someone drops his/her books or papers in the corridor, it is good manners to stop and help, especially when everyone is hustling to get to the next class.
11. When you see someone laden with parcels, or books, or something else, hold the door to let him/her get through.

12. Remember that most people whom you meet for the first time are inclined to like you, hoping that a new acquaintance will be somebody they like.
13. If you, as a young person, harbour doubts about how to behave during your first experience as a house guest, be yourself, and carry a small gift with you.
14. When you leave the bathroom, ensure that you leave it neater than you found it.
15. Join in family activities, as a house guest, even if you do not care much, for them.
16. Soft lighting, especially candlelight, can be flattering, providing a soothing atmosphere to what might otherwise be jarring.
17. A soft light helps camouflage cracking paints. It also makes people look less stressed.
18. Remember that giving a successful party depends upon your spirited attitude, and not on how much furniture or wealth you display.
19. Never apologise to people for what you did not do.
20. If you are giving a party, always be ready with a store of anecdotes or comments about something in the news that will ease a tense situation.
21. When you cater from outside and your maid breaks a plate or glass, do not attempt to take breakage cost out of her wages.
22. Never hesitate to entertain at 'odd' times — a breakfast party might be the best time to catch busy people.
23. Do not seat spouses or couples together.
24. Try to pair up a talker and a listener.

25. It is a gracious custom to serve coffee away from the table after dessert.
26. If you know that your guests smoke, put ash-trays and matches on the table.
27. The smokers should not even think about smoking until everyone has finished dessert.
28. Do not, when offered a dish at a friend's table, look at it critically, turn it about with the spoon and fork, and then refuse it.
29. Toasts should be long enough to cover the subject, but short enough to be amusing.
30. Remember when you dress up, that everything you put on communicates something, and your image is either working for or against you.
31. Sometimes a little is all the information you need to give about a person, especially if the title is something like "Doctor".
32. While introducing, if you are formal with one, do not be casual with the other.
33. Keep your drink in your left hand to avoid giving a wet, cold handshake.
34. Never stay behind your desk, when visitors arrive, unless you are planning to fire somebody!
35. Smile when you speak on the telephone because a smile can be 'heard' — your tone conveys you are smiling.
36. While using a voice mail, speak clearly, and make sure you know what you are going to say.
37. A smile relieves stress — so do smile at your colleagues.
38. When waiting for someone in a restaurant, stand where you can see the door without impeding traffic.

39. Never hitch up your sleeves as you sit down.
40. When acknowledging the news that a couple is engaged, tradition dictates that we congratulate the man, and wish the woman every happiness.
41. The most important factor in any sort of communication is that what you hear is more important than what I say — "I'm not sure I was clear about that" is much better than "You don't understand."
42. If your humorous retorts are frequently met with quizzical looks or strained smiles, leave jokes out of your speeches. You ca not tell a joke, and you should not.
43. Flowers are appropriate to send in the morning to a party, or the day after.
44. It is perfectly acceptable for a woman to send flowers to men.
45. If you are carrying wine or food to a dinner party, say something like, "We thought you might enjoy this later," thus relieving the host of the pressure of having to deal with the gift immediately.
46. "You" is a much better word than "I" for beginning a letter.
47. Use ink for a condolence letter or when replying to a formal invitation.

Faux Pas

1. It is contemptible to bring together recently separated or divorced persons with your other single friends, solely for the purpose of "fixing them up" with someone.
2. If things go wrong with the hired help, never criticise them in public.
3. A handshake is not a universally approved greeting.
4. "Look 'em right in the eye" is not always applicable.
5. What Americans call 'diapers' are called 'napkins' in England. This could lead to some hilarious or embarrassing misunderstandings.
6. Avoid sending alcohol to a person's office. Most companies prohibit alcohol consumption on the job.
7. Never send a gift to the office of an editor reporter, etc., to thank them for favourable publicity, as it looks more like a payoff.
8. Never carry away cutlery, bath towels, ash-trays, etc., from hotels where they are kept for the use of guests.
9. Nowadays, gallantry in the corporate culture will get you nowhere (as far as gender rules are concerned), except perhaps into hot water.
10. Never wear skirts and trousers that are so tight as to convey a message of sexiness.
11. Exposed cleavage and miniskirts are not appropriate business attire for a woman.

12. Do not give false compliments, and do not lie to people at social functions to be polite. People can detect your insincerity, no matter how well you act.
13. Do not ask for food or drink at a meeting unless they are being offered.
14. Printed thank-you cards or notes from a gift shop are not gestures acceptable as token of gratitude. Gratitude does not come pre-packaged.